BLIND MAN'S TOUCH

William Heyliger

Book 4 of the Stone and Lady Series

first published in 1935

Dr. Stone, reaching into the closet, found the gray suit that needed pressing. He knew it was gray because his fingers felt the three sharply-ridged lines of thread sewed on the inside of the collar. So, to the blind man, was every suit, shirt, tie and sock in his wardrobe marked for exact identification. One raised ridge of thread for blue, two for brown, and three for gray.

He came down the stairs with the suit. Joe Morrow had put a leash on Lady, and she whined eagerly.

"Ready to go, old girl?" The blind man patted the dog's head and took the leash. "All set, Joe? Got your money?"

"Yes, sir." The boy felt for the two dollars he had earned weeding a neighbor's garden. "I'll have fourteen dollars saved," he boasted.

"Wealth," the doctor chuckled, and snapped open his watch and touched the exposed hands with a finger. "We'll be back in time for dinner."

But that was a dinner they were destined never to eat.

Roses bloomed in the summer heat, fields of corn tasseled in the sun, and a dog ran out of a yard and barked at them furiously. Lady, intent only on the blind man in her keeping, pricked up her ears but did not change her rapid pace. The village was busy with its Saturday morning trade, and the tawny brute carefully maneuvered the doctor through the crowds. Joe clutched his two dollars and his bank-book. They left the gray suit at the tailor's and came out to the street. And at that moment a man, coatless and hatless, ran out of the Pelle Canning

Company building and went past them, panting.

Dr. Stone said: "Did you hear that man's breathing, Joe? He's frightened. Who is he?"

"Mr. Pelle," the boy told him.

"Where did he go?"

"Into the bank."

The doctor said: "Lady, right," and followed the dog across the roadway to the bank side of the street. A small door in one of the two-story brick buildings opened suddenly, and a girl hurried out. The door was marked: "OFFICE, MIDSTATE TEL. CO. UPSTAIRS," and the girl was Tessie Rich, one of the telephone operators. In her haste she almost ran into the blind man.

"Oh! I'm sorry, Doctor."

"No harm done, Tessie," Dr. Stone said, and chuckled slyly. "We're on our way to the bank. Any message you'd like me to give Albert Wall?"

The girl colored rosily. "I usually give him my own messages."

The wail of a siren filled the street and a police car went past them, traveling fast. Instantly the girl was across the sidewalk and through the telephone company door. The car stopped at the bank, and Joe saw a figure in blue uniform and brass buttons get out.

"Captain Tucker?" the blind man asked.

"Yes, Uncle David."

"The bank?"

"Yes, sir."

"Tessie gone? I see. And Tucker and Pelle both in a hurry." The doctor whistled an almost soundless whistle. "We'd better get on, Joe."

Something had gone wrong at the bank. The boy saw that at once. A score of depositors clung together in knots on the main floor, uneasy bank clerks stood behind the bronze grille of the teller's windows, and from some inner room came a roaring, bull voice shouting in anger. Bryan Smith, the president of the bank, agitated and flushed, appeared in the doorway of the little room, saw the blind man and cried out:

"Doctor! Doctor Stone! This way, please."

Joe Morrow, still clutching his two dollars and his

pass-book, went with his uncle and the dog, and the door closed upon them. Inside the room three men stood about the bank president's desk. The veins in Mr. Pelle's neck were swollen with rage; Albert Wall, the cashier, tapped his fingers against the desk and frowned, and a third man, who looked lost and bewildered, held on to the back of a chair near the window. This third man, whom Joe had never seen before, smelled of antiseptics and carried his right arm in a sling.

"Doctor," Bryan Smith sputtered, "this bank has been robbed of five thousand dollars. Robbed right under our noses. Not fifteen minutes ago."

"By whom?" the doctor asked quietly.

"We don't know. Somebody put a forged check through the window. At least Pelle says he signed only one check and—-"

"What do you mean I say I signed only one check?" the canner roared. "I tell you I signed only one. I should know! If you were fools enough to pay—-"

"But I telephoned you, Mr. Pelle," Albert Wall broke in. "You said—-"

"I know what I said. I told you I had given a check to Fred Hesset for five thousand dollars. If you paid five thousand dollars to another man on a forged check that's your funeral. The real Hesset is here." Mr. Pelle pointed to the man with bandaged arm. "Pay him."

"Not so fast," Bryan Smith fumed. "One check has been paid already. Now we have another and you say you signed only one. Which one?" The bank president held out two slips of paper.

Joe had a glimpse of them. Both were dated that day, both were made out to Fred Hesset, both were for five thousand dollars, both were signed "Paul Pelle." The canner stared at them for a long minute.

"This one," he said, and pushed one of the checks across the desk.

"How do you know?"

"Because this one is number 1046. I gave Hesset check No. 1046."

"How about your signature on this other check?"

"I tell you that isn't my signature."

With a quick movement the banker scrambled the checks and then laid them side by side partly covered by a blotter so that only the signatures showed.

"Now, Pelle," he snapped, "which one did you sign?"

The canner's neck swelled again. "What is this," he roared; "a trap? I can't tell them apart. That's what you're supposed to be able to do. I tell you—-"

"Gentlemen." Dr. Stone's voice was mild. "Let's stay with facts. As I understand it Pelle gave a man named Hesset a check for five thousand dollars this morning. What for?"

"Damages," Mr. Pelle snapped. "Hesset owns a butcher shop at Arlington. One of my trucks got out of control and skidded into the front of the shop. Hesset was caught in the wreckage; broken arm and broken collarbone. I don't carry liability insurance. I settled with him and gave him a check at eleven o'clock this morning."

Captain Tucker said: "Where does this second check come in?"

"Tell them, Albert," Bryan Smith ordered.

The cashier's fingers ceased to tap the desk. "At

11:13—I happened to glance at the clock—a man pushed a check through the window. It was a five thousand dollar check, made out to Fred Hesset and signed by Mr. Pelle. The man couldn't identify himself, so I called Mr. Pelle and was told he had given the check a few minutes before. I cashed it. Ten minutes later another Hesset check for five thousand dollars came through the window. It looked queer. I called Mr. Pelle again." Albert Wall made a gesture with his hands. "Then I telephoned for Captain Tucker."

The captain cleared his throat. "That first

check was the forged check?"

Again the cashier's hands moved. "So Mr. Pelle says."

The canner's face was livid. But before he could roar his wrath Dr. Stone's voice sounded quietly in the breathless tension of the room.

"May I see those checks?"

"Why—" The idea of sightless eyes trying to examine handwriting staggered Bryan Smith. "Why—why, of course, Doctor," he said weakly.

The checks crinkled faintly in the blind man's hands. Joe, watching his uncle's face, suddenly saw a sign that sent a hot needle through his spine. Tight, puckered lines had gathered around the sightless eyes.

"How many persons knew this check was to be paid today?" Dr. Stone asked.

"No one," Mr. Pelle answered shortly. "Things not connected directly with the buying and selling I keep to myself."

"But if you wrote Hesset surely your stenographer—-"

"I didn't write. I telephoned."

"When?"

"Last Monday evening–seven o'clock. I was alone in the office. I told him to be here promptly at eleven this morning."

Albert Wall said: "If you'll excuse me a moment—" and was gone. Joe felt the warning pressure of his uncle's foot upon his toe. The door of the inner room had not been tightly closed. Craning his neck, the boy saw the cashier at a telephone. Presently Albert Wall came back still with that slight frown upon his face.

"This thing was planned ahead," Captain Tucker said slowly.

"Forgery is always planned ahead," Dr. Stone agreed. "Somebody knew that at eleven this morning Pelle was to give Hesset a check. By the way, Pelle, when you telephoned

Monday evening did you tell Hesset what the amount of the check would be?"

"Certainly. No man settles a damage claim without knowing what he's going to get. I offered five thousand dollars; he accepted."

"So somebody knew three important facts—that you were going to pay a check at a certain time, the exact amount of the check and to whom it was to be made payable."

"Nobody knew it," the canner insisted.

"Except you and Hesset," the blind man said mildly.

The bandaged man, holding to the back of the chair, seemed to grow even more bewildered. Mr. Pelle's face was thrust across the desk.

"Doctor," he rasped, "are you insinuating—-"

Lady gave a low, deep-throated growl. One of the blind man's hands touched the tawny head.

"Pelle," he asked, "how did you come

to pick a Saturday morning to settle with Hesset?"

"Any law against it?" Mr. Pelle demanded.

"No." The doctor's voice was bland. "This is a small bank. It has only two really busy hours in the week. There is a rush from eleven to noon on Saturday just before the week-end closing; another rush from eight to nine Monday morning with business men coming in with their Saturday cash. During the week there would be leisure for a cashier to scrutinize a man; perhaps to telephone and ask, among other things, for a description. But on Saturday, after eleven, there is pressure and haste. And in this hour of pressure a check went through."

Mr. Pelle wet his lips nervously. Captain Tucker stood very still.

"Anything else, Doctor?" he asked.

"Why, yes." The blind man took a pipe from his pocket and filled it slowly. "Why did Hesset bring his check here to be cashed? Why didn't he take it back to Arlington and deposit it in his own bank?"

"Well, Hesset?" the police captain barked.

Joe saw the bandaged man grip the back of the chair with his good hand. "I know nothing about two checks, Captain. I saw only one check. I wanted the money in my pocket. Cash is cash. Sometimes a check you think is good—-"

Mr. Pelle's roar filled the room. "You dare say that to me, Hesset?" Captain Tucker sprang between the two men, and Joe shrank out of the way. Dr. Stone said: "I had better take the dog out of here. Come, Joe." It was long past noon, and the bank was closed. Albert Wall went with them down the long, deserted floor to open the front door and let them out.

"What do you make of this?" he asked in an undertone.

"Pelle?" the doctor asked mildly.

The cashier hesitated. "Well—yes.

Five thousand dollars is a lot of money. I know the condition of Pelle's account; business hasn't been any too good of late and five thousand dollars might hit him hard. If he could pay five thousand dollars with one hand and manipulate a forged check with the other and get five thousand dollars back from the bank–. For that, though, he'd need a confederate, somebody to go to the window with the first check. It doesn't seem probable."

"A possibility though," the blind man said. "A great many possibilities," he added. "Let's not forget Hesset. Either Hesset or Pelle could have worked this with a confederate. Or some person, unknown and unsuspected, might be the criminal. Good day, Albert." He held out his hand.

"Good-bye, Doctor." Their hands met. The heavy door of the bank closed.

The puckered lines had come back to the sightless eyes. Man, boy and dog came down the stone steps of the old-fashioned building. On the sidewalk the doctor spoke.

"Joe, you could see them. How did Pelle strike you?"

"He was wild," the boy answered.

"A man may protest too much or too little," the blind man observed dryly. "Hesset?"

"He was scared."

"So! That leaves Albert Wall. Could you see him when he left the room?"

"Yes, sir."

"Where did he go?"

"To a telephone."

"Good lad!" The doctor knocked the ashes from his pipe and walked beside the dog in silence.

"The telephone office," he said suddenly.

Joe wondered what unseen tangent of the case could bring them there. They went up a narrow mountain of a stairway. Lady, leading, slowed and swung her Master to the left, stopping him at the counter.

"Can you tell me," Dr. Stone asked, "what operators were on duty at seven o'clock last Monday night?"

"We have only one girl on duty after 6:45," the manager told him, and consulted a record. "That was Tessie Rich's night. Any complaint, Doctor?"

"Merely a matter of information," the doctor smiled. Back in the sunlight Joe saw that the smile was gone and that the puckers around the sightless eyes had become intent. Dr. Stone said absently: "You must be hungry, Joe," and they went toward a restaurant. But before they reached it there was a rush of feet and a woman's breathless voice.

"Doctor!" It was Tessie Rich. "Why did you want to know if I was on duty last Monday night?"

"I didn't."

"Oh!" The girl was nonplused. "But–but you asked—-"

"I asked who was on duty," the doctor said

gently. "Did you have any reason to think I was asking about you?"

Subtle, hidden undertones filled the question, and the hot needle was again in Joe's spine. The girl raised a handkerchief to her lips.

"Why—why, of course not, Doctor? Why should I?" There was something of hysterical panic in her voice.

"Why?" the blind man asked, blandly.

In the restaurant Joe Morrow chewed on food that all at once stuck in his throat. Why had his uncle gone to the telephone office? What hidden spring had that visit touched and what had frightened

Tessie Rich? Were Mr. Pelle and the girl both involved? Had the canner actually signed two checks? What about Mr. Hesset? Who had gone to the bank with the first check and walked out with five thousand dollars in cash?

"Do you know who did it, Uncle David?"

A pipe came out of a pocket; blue smoke spiraled fragrantly about a face that had become placid and bland.

"Joe, the bank is built on a corner—at an angle to the corner. How far up the street can you see?"

"Quite a distance."

"As far as Pelle's factory?"

"Yes, sir."

"I know who didn't do it," the blind man said, and stood up. "And," he added quietly, "I think I know who did."

Joe hoped it wasn't Tessie Rich. They walked out of the village and up along the dirt road. The doctor said aloud: "If I could pick one more link–" and left the sentence unfinished and said no more. Tree toads made metallic clamor in the afternoon heat, and the earth smelled as though it were baked.

A clock struck three as they entered the house. Dr. Stone paced the porch and Lady stretched off in a patch of sun and watched him steadily. Joe brought up a tool from the cellar and prepared to trim the hedge.

A light delivery truck stopped in the road and a young man carried a suit up to the house.

"You're prompt," Dr. Stone said. The suit was on a hanger; the coat brushed against his knee with a soft crinkle. He ran one hand into a pocket and pulled out a paper. Strange! There had been nothing in the pockets of the suit he had carried away. His hand went up quickly to feel inside the collar. The three sharply ridged lines of thread were not there.

"Joe!" he called. "Stop that tailor's boy—-" But the

driver had already discovered his mistake. He came up the walk with the suit of gray. Joe laid down the clippers and followed him in.

"I'll carry that up to your room, Uncle Da—-What's Lady got?"

The dog had found a paper on the floor. Now she carried it to the doctor. It crinkled in his hand.

It was a small paper, no larger than half a sheet from a note-book. Joe watched those hands move, gently exploring, over every inch of surface. And as the hands moved, Dr. Stone's face changed. Joe had seen that sharp, alert expression before.

It was a silent sign that, some place in the eternal darkness of his world, the blind man had found light.

"Joe, there is writing on this paper?"

"Yes, sir." The boy looked closer and drew in a hot, throbbing breath. "Uncle David! The same thing's written all over it. Paul

Pelle, Paul Pelle, Paul Pelle."

Dr. Stone said a soft: "Ah!" and folded the paper and put it in his pocket. "The criminal always slips," he observed; "there's always something forgotten." He stood for a moment whistling softly. "Care to stretch your legs? I want a word with the tailor."

Joe's eyes, fascinated, were on the writing. That paper had fallen from the suit delivered by mistake, and now his uncle wanted to know to whom the suit belonged.

"Couldn't you telephone him, Uncle David?"

The blind man's mouth twitched. "The call might pass

through Tessie's switchboard," he said dryly.

The boy groped, and stumbled, and sought to find the meaning. The afternoon sun was low; the first cool breath of evening breeze blew over the dirt road. He waited outside while his uncle talked with the tailor; when the man came out he was whistling.

"Police station," he said.

Captain Tucker was at his desk. "Doctor," he burst out, "this thing is baffling. Lay those two checks side by side and you can't tell the signatures apart. I've talked to New York. There isn't a forger known to the police in this part of the country."

Dr. Stone asked: "Did Albert Wall give you a description?"

"Of the man who cashed that first check? A lot of good that does. Five feet eight, about 155 pounds, dark, clean-shaven, blue suit. It fits a million men."

"It would," the doctor said blandly. His face was inscrutable. "You heard Pelle's story and Albert Wall's. Get statements prepared."

"For what?"

"For them to sign." His hands felt along the desk for the telephone and he called Bryan Smith's house. "Bryan? Dr. Stone. Do you know where you can find Albert at this hour? He's with you now? Can you have him at the bank in an hour? I'll be along with Captain Tucker and Pelle." He put down the telephone. "You have an hour, Tucker, in which to get those statements ready and dig up Pelle. He's probably at the factory."

"But why signed statements?" Captain Tucker demanded impatiently.

"Bait," the blind man said casually. "Sometimes you use cheese in a trap; sometimes you use printed words." He settled into a chair and closed his eyes, and appeared to doze. The dog, ever watchful, lay at his feet.

Captain Tucker left the room, and presently, in another part of the police station, a typewriter began to click. The captain came back grumbling and out-of-sorts. The doctor's devious, subtle methods always provoked him to a show of ill-humor.

The telephone rang sharply—there had been an automobile crash near the bridge. A minute later a motor roared into life in the alley beside the station and a motorcycle patrolmen sped away. The blind man did not stir.

Joe Morrow squirmed restlessly and watched the clock.

Mr. Pelle arrived in a chastened, subdued mood; a uniformed man brought Captain Tucker several typewritten sheets; the wall clock struck the hour, and Dr. Stone opened his eyes.

"Ready, Tucker?"

They drove to the bank in the police car. Bryan Smith let them in. Dusk had begun to gather in the corners farthest from the windows, a guardlight burned in front of the steel safe, and a burst of ceiling lights shone from the inner room. Captain Tucker and Mr. Pelle went on ahead while the bank president saw to it that the door was securely locked. The doctor lingered.

"Bryan," he said softly, "are there pens and ink on your desk?"

"Certainly."

"Remove them; Lady, forward." And before the man could reply the doctor was on his way past the teller's cages, one hand holding the harness-grip, his body bent a little toward the guiding dog.

Bryan Smith, saying that they might need room, cleared the desk. Mr. Pelle's eyes shifted from side to side and missed nothing. Albert Wall seemed to wait patiently the outcome of this strange gathering. But what held Joe's attention and sent the blood pounding in his veins was a something that lay behind the passive placidity of his uncle's face.

"Captain Tucker," Dr. Stone said, "has prepared statements for Pelle and Albert to sign. You have pens, gentlemen? Now, if you will sign them—-"

Albert Wall read rapidly and, taking a fountain pen from his pocket, signed at once. Mr. Pelle read his paper through and then read it again. He wrote his name slowly.

"Albert's paper, Captain." The doctor laid it on the desk at his right hand. "Pelle's." It went upon the left. "Now, Bryan, if I may have those checks. First the one Pelle says he didn't sign." It went upon the right with Albert Wall's statement.

The bank president's nerves had been under a long strain. "What's the meaning of this, Doctor?" he snapped. "If you have your suspicions, let us know them. If you have anything to say, say it. Don't waste time."

"Presently," the doctor said mildly. His hands had moved, mysteriously explored, and had come to rest. That vague something in his face was no longer there; he was serene. When he spoke again his voice was almost confidential. "Had that fountain pen long, Albert?"

The cashier was surprised. "Four or five years."

"You kept it too long. It tripped you."

"Tripped? Look here, Doctor, what are you driving at?"

"Money," the blind man said. "Five thousand dollars. What did you do with it?"

In the appalled silence of the room Joe heard clearly the sound of someone breathing with an effort. The cashier had not moved.

"Do you know what you're saying, Doctor?"

"Quite," the doctor said pleasantly. From his pocket he drew out a paper. "Did you ever see this?"

It was the paper Lady had picked from the floor. Albert Wall's eyes widened.

"A dangerous business, handling money," Dr. Stone mused. "Thousands upon thousands of dollars pouring through one's hands every day. Other people's money. If a man has a weak spot some place inside it may get him—a fever to have some of this money for his own. If the right moment comes, or the right scheme presents itself—-

"You heard about the settlement Pelle was to make with Hesset, didn't you, Albert? The weak spot took control. You saw a chance to put your hands on five thousand dollars so cleverly that it would never be traced to you. You must have spent hour upon hour practicing Pelle's signature. And finally you had a check that you thought was perfect.

"You could see Pelle's factory. Saturday morning you saw Hesset go in. You may have gone to

Arlington so you'd know what he looked like; you may have figured you'd know him because he would be bandaged. You saw him come out; you waited a minute or two. Then you telephoned Pelle that a man was at the window with a five thousand dollar check. Naturally Pelle said it was all right. You knew he'd say that. Hadn't he just given the check? So you stamped 'paid' on the check you had forged, and placed it with the checks the bank had cashed that morning. Shortly thereafter the real Hesset appeared and you telephoned Pelle again. Oh, it was a sweet scheme, Albert. Apparently there was no come-back. Hadn't

Pelle told you to pay the first check? Could the bank be held responsible for paying a check Pelle told it to pay? In its simplicity the plan was almost genius. But–" The doctor paused. "You slipped."

The cashier had not moved. "Doctor," he said evenly, "your story is preposterous. You heard Pelle say he was alone in the office when he telephoned Hesset. To put a scheme like this through I would have to know in advance that a settlement had been made, when a check was to be given, and for how much. How could I know it?"

"Bryan," the blind man said, "will you call the telephone office and ask them can they send Tessie Rich over here for a moment?"

The bank president reached for the telephone.

"Don't do that," Albert Wall called sharply. In a moment all the self-control had gone out of him. There was a chair behind him; he reached back and sank into it heavily. "Keep her out of it," he said in a whisper. "I–I did it. I alone."

Mr. Pelle wiped beads of sweat from his forehead. "I thought you suspected me, Doctor?"

"It is wise, sometimes, to

appear to suspect the innocent. Do you remember I asked for the checks this morning? A moment later I knew you were not the man. As soon as you said you had telephoned Hesset a significant thing happened. Albert left the room. He went to a telephone. My guess is he went there to warn Tessie not to tell anybody she had spoken to him about the Hesset settlement."

The cashier lifted a white face. "How did you know that?"

"Deduction. One person could have heard what Pelle said to Hesset—the central operator through whom the call passed. When I left here Albert took me to the door. I made a point of shaking hands with him. A cashier who had just paid a forged check, it is only natural to suppose, would be nervous and upset. Albert's hand was hard and strained, his grip that of a man steeled to see something through..... What?

"I stopped at the telephone office

and asked what girls had been on duty at seven o'clock Monday evening. Tessie had been on duty alone. I did not mention her name; and yet, before I had gone one hundred feet, she was out in the street after me, badly shaken, demanding to know why I had inquired about her. That end of the picture was complete.

Tessie and Albert were sweethearts; she had told him of the Pelle call in confidential gossip. I knew then who the guilty man was, but I could not prove it.

"This afternoon the tailor delivered me another man's suit by mistake. I found it was Albert's. This was in one of the pockets."

The doctor pushed across the desk the paper covered with the canner's signature. "Probably every other paper on which Albert had practiced the signature had been destroyed–this one had been overlooked. As he could not have practiced forgery at the bank he must have done it at home. And as the same pen had written the signatures on this paper and the signature on the forged check, they must have been written, not with a bank pen, but with a pen that Albert carried with him. I wanted to have him use that pen before witnesses.

"So I had Captain Tucker prepare

statements and bring you here. I had Bryan clear the desk so that Albert would have no other pen to use but his own. Once he signed that statement he had damned himself."

Bryan Smith, examining the two checks, shook his head. "Doctor, you cannot see. How could you tell that?"

"Have you a magnifying glass?" the blind man asked.

The bank president took one from a drawer.

"Examine the check Pelle signed and the statement he signed. Both signatures are smooth. Look at the forged check. There are three l's in Paul Pelle. On each of the three upstrokes on the l's the pen gouged the paper a bit. Here's the paper that was in the suit. The same gouge on the upstrokes. Now the statement Albert Wall signed. There are also three l's in his name, and the same gouge on the upstrokes. All made by the same pen."

Joe Morrow was filled with a sense of pride

and wonder. Bryan Smith said slowly:

"Doctor, I fail to see how you, sightless, could detect that."

"Eyes," Dr. Stone said. "Auxiliary eyes. When sight goes, other senses quicken." He laid his hands upon the table, palms up, and the light shone upon the delicate, sensitive finger tips.

"You mean you could feel these grooves?" Captain Tucker demanded.

"Yes."

The captain ran his own fingers across the signatures. "I don't see how," he complained. "I don't feel a thing."

Dr. Stone filled his pipe with expert care. "You are not blind," he said mildly. "You lack a blind man's touch."

ABOUT THE AUTHOR

William Heyliger was a prolific author of books for readers of all ages. He wrote baseball stories in "The St. Mary's Series." His blind detective, Dr. David Stone has provided joy and inspiration to many. He died in 1955.

ABOUT THE COVER

The image on the cover is adapted from a poster for the 1925 film *Wild Justice*, starring the dog, Peter the Great. Only the advertisements remain, the orginal film has been lost.

MORE BOOKS AT:

superlargeprint.com

KEEP ON READING!

OBLIGATORY TINY PRINT: This story is in the public domain and published here under fair use laws. The Super Large Print logo is copyright of Super Large Print. The cover design may not be reproduced for commercial purposes. If you have questions or believe we've made a mistake, please let us know at superlargeprint@gmail.com. And thank you for helping this book find its way to a person who might appreciate it.

The cover is adapted from a poster for the 1925 film Wild Justice. (CC BY-SA 3.0)
This book is set in a font designed by Abelardo Gonzalez called OpenDyslexic

ISBN 9798741064337

Made in the USA
Monee, IL
20 June 2024